wind dancing

robert a kamarowski

and we did speak only to break
the silence of the sea!

samuel taylor coleridge
the rime of the ancient mariner

hemingway was out here

the captain sits on the shady side of the boat with his
back to the cabin and his legs stretched along the
deck   a soiled greek fishermans cap sits on his lap and
his eyes look out over the sea from a face made leathery
by the sun

maybe right here   maybe right on this spot
fishin en drinkin   en maybe writin   en maybe
fuckin   right here   right here where we drift

the cuban looks at the haitian and smiles   his teeth are
large and straight and shiny and give his face a childlike
glow

you gonna tell us all bout hemingway agin capn

the captain scratches the stubble on his face and then
places his hands behind his head

    it dont matter what you two think anyway   he was
    a hell of a man a real man   even if he was a writer

the haitian smiles now too   his crooked yellow teeth are
framed by thin lips and his dark eyes are surrounded by
skin so black it looks blue

    *how many times we got to hear dis
    cahptane*

    many time as I wanna tell it   a hunerd more
    time if I want   im gonna say it again   right
    here   right here he coulda been

the haitian winks at the cuban

    *have you ever read anyting by him
    cahptane*

the captain looks at the haitian and then returns his blue
eyes to the sea

    you know I read im   got the book in my cabin
    you seen it there plenty a time   old man en
    the sea   best book ever wrote

wind dancing

the haitian winks again at the cuban

what else you read by him cahptane

the captain hesitates

nothin   dont have to   that ones goodnuff for a
lifetime

*if you do not read him how do you
know what he might be doing
out here*

theres plenty a stuff at the key bout im   you
know that   i even read an article in a paper
once   en a guy used to own the rosy bell who
read ever book he ever wrote told me all kindsa
stuff bout im   i know plenty bout hemingway
dont you worry   I know plenty

*you sure you read deh book
cahptane   not any pictures in it
you know*

the cubans eyes are wide as he places a finger to his
pursed lips   a heavy sigh deserts him

watch yer step man   you dont wanna cross that

3

line   I aint gotta lie ta no one   specially the
likes a you two   you watch yer step man

the captain looks at his cap   he rubs a spot of grease and
the stain spreads and discolors his thumb   then he
raises his head and shades his eyes and squints out over
the ocean but the sun is behind him and there is nothing
at sea to watch

you be careful there man   theres plenty more
where you two come from   theres plenty a
help waitin back at the key

the cuban covers his smile with his hand

I don say nutn capn   that not me sayin nutn

you dont never say nothin   but I know you two
playin that winkin game a yers

a mound of water tunnels under the boat raising the men
up and then lowering them back down

a gull crosses the sky

two clouds hold each other as they dance above the sea
and water breaks off the port side of the boat when
something surfaces while feeding

wind dancing

the cuban continues to smile as he returns to swabbing
the deck   the mop is frail in his large hands and the
massive muscles roll across his shining back as he attacks
an oil spot   a spanish song comes from his lips in a
sweet voice that is surprising for his size

the haitian reads a book   his pince nez are stuck to his
nose and the gold circular rims reflect the sun off his
deep black face   his lips move as the words cross his
eyes but he lets no sound escape his mouth   a small
hand that used to be delicate but is now calloused moves
a page from one side of the book to the other

returning his eyes to the sea the captain runs a hand over
his smooth tanned head until he reaches the short gray
hairs at the back and rubs them to enjoy the tingling
feeling   his feet are bare and his dirty white pants are
rolled up half way between the ankle and the knee   the
hairs on his chest are gray and long and climb out of his
open shirt   he settles his head against the cabin and
closes his eyes and with the cubans voice as background
music drifts easily to sleep

you done a fair job on the deck

the cuban looks up surprised and smiles his wonderful
smile

after chewing his sandwich the haitian swallows   takes a
sip of beer and wipes his mouth

    daht must mean you cleaned deh boat
    cleaner den a hospital   maybe we
    can eat off deh deck

    i tell im its a fair job en you gotta make somethin
    a it

    you pretty scarce wit deh
    compliment cahptane

maybe cause the work aint always worth
complementin   en you been speakin yer mind
pretty good lately man   must be cuz we gettin
closer to gettin yer people

might be cahptane   might be
and you have been reading my mind
lately   must be all doze books
you been reading

the cuban puts his hand over his smile but even the
captain grins at this and takes a long draught of his beer
and breaks into a short laugh   he shakes his head

you aint never lost fer words   maybe you a
perfesser after all

oh i am not a professor
cahptane   i never was   back in
haiti i was a school teacher at a
small school in de interior   i
taught children to read and
write   i was never a professor
but i always felt important
children are deh future
cahptane   deh future of haiti
  deh future of deh world

the captain takes another drink and wipes his mouth

with the back of his hand and looks at the haitian and
then turns his gaze out to sea

> i aint never had much use fer teachers myself
> just think they bettern ever one else   en always
> lookin ta make ya feel low

> oh daht not me cahptane   daht not
> me   i always love deh children
> and try to help dem whenever i
> could   daht may be deh trouble
> cahptane   you never had me for a
> teacher

they all smile at this

> well you talkin real pretty and you always lookin
> down at ever body from behind those fancy
> glasses a yers

> my glasses come from my
> granfadder   deze glasses were his
> and he give dem to my fadder and my
> fadder give dem to me

the haitian removes the glasses and cradles them with
both hands

> i remember one night as a child my

fadder was reading me my most
special story   i see he has a
tear running out from under deze
very glasses   he put deh book
down and tell me my granfadder died
daht dey   i just sat dehr a
moment   i was a child you see
and den i cry like a little baby
because i understand i will no
longer see daht crazy old crooked
face anymore

the ocean presses its back to the boat raising the men for a moment and then letting them back down

the haitian places the glasses back on his nose

deze glasses correct our vision
perfectly when reading   is not
daht amazing cahptane   my
granfadder my fadder and me each
have perfect vision for reading wit
deh same pair of glasses

the captain shifts his weight and stares at the sea   he removes his cap and rubs his head

i still aint never had much use fer teachers myself

wind dancing

a breeze passes over the earth pushing wrinkles of water
across the ocean and giving life to a shirt that hangs from
the lifeline

the captain finishes eating and takes the rest of his beer to
the bow where he sits and looks south toward the distant
equator

moving to the starboard side of the boat where he laid a
line out to dry the cuban begins to coil it around his arm
as another song comes to his lips

the haitian puts his beer down on the deck   he coats the
pince nez with mist from his mouth and begins to clean
the lenses with the tail of his shirt

the boat rolls slowly under the three men and the ocean
stretches out unblemished in all directions   the blue
sky is dotted with clouds that refuse to move and the sun
drops mica into the sea   gulls circle three or four times
overhead and then wheel and flee to the north

why dont you come in deh wadder
cahptane

the haitian and the cuban swim in the clear green sea

the captain looks at them   he takes his cap off and
scratches his head

come in deh wadder   it is
wonderful for swimming

water feel good capn

the captain looks down at the men and at the sea that
stretches blue and green to the horizon   he checks his
watch and looks around the boat

maybe i will

he drops his cap on the deck and then removes his shirt
and shoes

> you aint got no hard on waitin under the water
> for me now do ya

the cuban laughs

the haitian looks hurt

> *i am very sorry cahptane but i do*
> *not   i ahm not daht way*

the cuban laughs again

> that aint what i mean   you know i only kiddin
> here but you always gotta twist things around
> dont ya   you a perfesser if i ever seen one all
> right

the captain removes the rest of his clothes and jumps into
the sea   the deeper he sinks the faster his heart beats so
he claws his way to the surface and breaths heavily   he
treads water with short uneven strokes and his eyes are
wide and dart across the ocean keeping track of the
men   he remains close to his boat

the cuban swims away   his long stroke carries him
farther and farther out to sea until it seems he will be

lost   finally he stops and turns and waves to the captain
and the haitian before swimming back to the boat

the haitian bobs up and down letting the water wash over
his head and run in and out of his mouth   the sea clings
to his short curly hair in fat drops and scatters in all
directions as he shakes his head and laughs

the men tread water and talk as the sea caresses their
bodies and the sun pricks their heads with needles of
heat   first the cuban goes up the ladder and then the
haitian and finally the captain climbs out of the sea
there is no one around for miles so they stand naked in
the sun and dry their hair and wipe the water from their
eyes and wrap the towels around their waists   they sit
and drink and shade their eyes from the sun but there is
little talk   hillocks of sea pass under the boat and gulls
circle overhead and soon the men dress and each man
goes to his own spot on the boat where the silence is
more comfortable

sitting with his back to the cabin and his cap on his legs
and his eyes closed the captain rubs a hand across his
face   he crosses one foot over the other

the haitian finds a triangle of shade in the cockpit and
sets the pince nez on his nose and continues his silent
pronunciation of each word on each page of the
shadowline by conrad   his finger runs along each page
leading his eyes and lips to the next word and he stops

and smiles a moment thinking how in another life he
would scold his students for this same habit

with a panama hat tipped over one eye the cuban works
on a piece of deck where the paint has come up   he
scrapes and sands and doesnt seem to notice the heat that
pours onto his back and glazes his skin with sweat   a
dolphin rises from the water and the cuban looks at its
bright eye and smiles and feels everything will be
okay   everything will be okay tomorrow night and
beyond he is certain of that now

and then the dolphin submerges and is seen no more

daht one lonely man dehr

the haitian tosses his chin at the captain who lies on the
port side with his cap covering his eyes and a bottle of
beer cupped between his hands   a deep rumble departs
his lips as his thick chest rises and falls rises and falls
lifting the bottle skyward each time he inhales

the capn   you thin the capn lonely

shhh   you do not want to wake him up
let deh man sleep   but i tell you deh
more i talk to him and deh more i watch
him deh more i see a lonely man dehr

an itinerant wave passes under the boat and continues on
toward africa

he does not talk about a wife   he
does not talk about a woman
he does not talk about children he
does not talk about anyting but his
boat   his boat and
fishing   and hemingway   i tink
daht a very lonely man lying
over dehr

the cuban looks up confused and his smile abandons him

i don   i don think so   he a tough man that
capn   i don think he lonely less he wannabe

maybe maybe   but i tink daht
one lonely man

whatre you two dreamin up back there

good afternoon cahptane   how was
your sleep

my sleep was good en that aint what i asked you
two   i aint heard such whisperin since i was
a kid

we did not want to wake you up
cahptane   we wanted to let you
sleep

the captain rises and stretches his arms to the sky and places his cap on his head   he rubs a hand over his growing beard and scratches under his chin   his chest has a clump of wet hairs where the bottle rested and now each drop reflects the sun at different angles as he walks aft   his pants have dropped below his wide navel and the weathered belt has come undone and hangs limply framing his crotch and swinging in time with his gait

  he scratches under his arm   he lowers himself to the cockpit and tosses the empty bottle over the side sending a band of circular rings radiating over the ocean that become larger and larger until they disappear under the strain of their own size   he sits on the gunwale and removes his cap   he runs a hand over his head and then adds the sweat to the accumulating history on his pants he looks up at the sky

    that humiditys comin   i can feel it   the
    weathers been kind to us so far but i can tell you
    that humiditys comin

the cuban looks at the captain and brings the smile back to his face

weather feelin okay to me capn

    you cant hardly tell the diffrence now but i know
    its startin   itll be here tanight or tamarrah   i
    dont know which but itll be here

if you ever quit fishing cahptane
you can be a wehder man   maybe be
on deh tv and telling people   oh
daht humidity is coming daht
humidity is coming

the cuban laughs behind his hand

capn gonna fish forever   right capn

i dont know how long itll be that i keep fishin but
i know one damn thing en thats that i wont be on
no tv talkin shit bout the weather like this crazy
man here thinks   you got crazy idears en a lotta
space between those ears for a perfesser

a line of clouds forms a bridge over the ocean and the
suns rays assail the men from an ever lower angle
another mysterious swell of water that spawns from
nowhere ploughs under the boat raising the starboard
side first and then the port side and then moves away
the horizon is a line of contrasting blues that is precise
and flawless and unending

flying fish dance across the water to feel the suns warmth
for a moment and then plunge back into the safety and
coolness of the sea

a tern points its bright orange beak to the south and
swings back and forth as though pulled by opposite

wind dancing

strings   it hovers above as though looking for
something lost until it finally falls toward the sea in a
suicidal plunge   the bird gathers speed as it drops only
to break its fall inches above the water and then fly away
to its home on an island far to the northeast

daht sun look like it is on fire

look like a round ball   a basketball don it capn

looks like a fireball droppin down ta hell gonna
set all those pour souls on fire down there

*how can you say daht cahptane   it
is a beautiful sunset and you tink
of hell now*

its a free sun en ever man can think what he
wants of it

the captain stares at the haitian

well   aint that the truth

daht deh troot cahptain   daht deh
troot   but dis is not heaven and
hell right now   dis is deh world
and it is a wonderful sunset for us
to enjoy

they continue eating and drinking but each man holds
his eyes to the sun as it drops to its waist and ignites the
sky   the earth is draped in a blanket of scarlet from
horizon to horizon   the sky tarnishes the sea with
pockets of blood that change to ink then back to blood

a pod of dolphins rise out of the water   their black
outlines cross the sun and reenter the sea and rise again
black and distant and return for good into the burning
ocean as silently as they appeared

the cuban is smiling   he places his food and drink on
the deck and stands and walks to the starboard gunwale
to be closer to the falling star and its spikes of majestic
light   with one hand he holds the lifeline and with the
other he scratches his shoulder but his eyes never release
the sunset

at last the sun loses its struggle with the evening and
disappears below the horizon but refuses to surrender
completely   a funnel of light still touches the sky and
burns the motionless clouds that fall in its path   what
was blue and scarlet is now red and orange and yellow
with shades between

and then darkness slides across the earth   not total and
black but a gray indecision   a hesitant shadow
grudgingly emerges as the sun dissolves and when the
last rays of light finally evaporate lowers its heavy
blanket onto the three men

the cuban returns to his food   he eats with the heartiness
of a boy and his eyes walk from the captain to the haitian
to the deck to the sky and a smile works its way to his
face even as he chews

the haitian holds a sandwich to his mouth but does not
make a move to eat   he only stares at the fading horizon

the captain manipulates a bite of food to his right cheek
and mixes some beer with it and then swallows audibly

   that was some sunset tanight   my heads seen a
   lotta sunsets but it dont recall one like that bafore

   makes a man believe deh world is
   special does it not cahptane

   the world is special   aint no doubt god put us
   here when you see that   aint no doubt at all

i did not know you were so
religious cahptane

the captain scratches his beard and turns a bottle of beer
against his lips and wipes the back of his hand across
his face

    i aint no church goer but i know when things er
    sent down from above fer people ta see

    and you tink god sent daht sunset
    down for you to see

    sent down for all us ta see   you seen it too didnt
    ya   aint no other reason for somethin so
    beautiful to be seen on this sorry place

    why is not every sunset so
    beautiful den

the captain looks toward the haitian

    maybe for the same reason i aint always
    complimentin the work round here   cause we
    aint worth it all the time

    could not it be just deh sun and
    clouds and sea coming togedder to
    make a sunset like daht

the captain wipes his lips across his shoulder

    youre makin no sense ta me   a course its the sun
    and sea and those clouds all creatin that sunset
      but its gotta be put together by somethin
    dont it

    whatre you tryin ta say there man

the haitian puts his bottle on the gunwale and shifts his
weight

the captain takes a drink of beer

    well   aint ya got nothin ta say   this here
    might be a day ta ramember if youre dumb
    struck

a wave rocks the boat causing the haitian to grab his beer

    i do not know cahptane   i am not
    as sure as i once was about deh
    world

    didnt you used ta teach in a cathlic school aint
    that what you said   and now it sounds like yer
    tellin me ya dont believe in god

the captain turns to the cuban

well dont this make ya wanna wet yer pants
    mister perfesser here teachin kids about god
when he dont believe in god imself

the captain rubs the bottle in his hands

    still aint got nothin ta say   maybe you aint so
    smart after all

the cuban stands

    you still thin the humidty comin capn

    we aint talkin humidity now man   at least i
    aint   its about sunsets en god en teachin kids
    stuff ya dont believe yerself

a light breeze passes its fingers over the men and water
breaks off the bow and gulls fly unseen to the west

the captain looks at the outline of the haitian who stares
down at the deck

    you been readin so many books ya got yer head
    all screwed up en cant see things thatre plain
    as day

the haitian finishes his beer and leans into the cabin to

toss the empty bottle into the trash   he returns to the cockpit and gazes up at the emerging stars

i am not so sure of deh world
anymore cahptane   deh world or deh
rest of what life is   my fait was
very deep and very real and very
pure until my wife died and deh coup
cahptane   my wife was coming home
and stopped to talk to deh woman at
one of deh market stalls and a man
who had been drinking runs off deh
road and hits her and crushes her
and kills her   i wonder a very
long time about daht   i wonder
why she was taken from me   i come
to know daht i am being selfish to
tink daht way but i cannot help it
until one day i tink past just me
and wonder why she is taken away
from all deh udder people daht loved
her smile and her warm hands   why
does dis happen   and if it
is her time to go to heaven why does
it happen in such a violent way
why not in her sleep   i begin to
wonder about deze tings and do not
feel good tinking about dem but my

```
head does what it wants and tinks
what it wants        so i go back to
work and my students and start to
live again and den deh coup comes
and people are beaten and dragged
away        and now i do not know
cahptane          i do not know
```

the captain takes his cap off and rubs his head

> well you aint the only ones had a run a bad luck
> en it dont make ever one go leavin god en makin
> their lives inta feelin sorry for emselves   ya
> gotta hang on ta somethin

the captain tosses an empty beer bottle over the side and
retrieves another from the cooler on deck   he walks to
the bow and sits with his legs dangling over the side and
a hand holding onto a stanchion

the cuban lets out a deep sigh and walks over to the
gunwale where earlier he had watched the blazing sun
and now listens to the black ocean move steadily
under him

the haitian walks to the bow and sits on a hatch above the
captain and looks at the dotted sky

```
and what about you cahptane        why
is your fait so strong      you do
```

wind dancing

not have a wife or children daht
anyone knows about   are not doze
deh tings to be happy about

the captain sets the beer between his legs and rolls up the
sleeves of his shirt   he picks at a scab on the back of one
of his fingers and tosses it into the sea and turns and faces
the haitian but remains silent save for a clicking noise he
makes with his tongue   he returns his gaze to the sea

he scans the emptiness for several long seconds and then
looks at the haitian once more

> i aint gotta say nothin ta you   i aint gotta
> explain nothin ta you   i dont have a wife en
> never have en never will   theres more ta life
> then a wife en kids   en even if i wanted a
> family it aint ever mans cut out for that stuff
> some just aint made ta do it en is best left by
> themselves en thats just what i done instead a
> feelin sorry for myself bout somethin like
> you done

the sound of the cuban rummaging around the cockpit
drifts up to the two men

well you may be right about daht
cahptane   you may be right   but
i do not feel i feeling sorry for

31

myself   i am just looking at deh
world differently den i was in
deh past

the cuban joins the captain and the haitian on the
bow   the sea supports the men in its unpredictable
hands as the stars climb high overhead and the night
claims ownership of the earth

i told ya that humidity was comin didnt i

the captain shoulders his way out of the cabin and climbs onto the deck   he is shirtless and barefoot and his pants are wet around the waist as he looks up at the darkening sky and runs a frayed bandanna across his head

you was right capn   feel like soup out here

you are a born wehder man
cahptane   you will be on deh tv
some day   i can tell you now you
will be on deh tv

i aint got time fer yer shit now man

he runs the bandanna across the back of his neck and then places the cap on his head god damn but there wont be no sleepin tanight

even when deh wehders good we dont
sleep deh night before a pickup
have you not noticed daht cahptane

the captain looks at the gray form of the haitian who has
dragged his thin mattress out on deck and is lying on it
with his head propped against a ball of clothes supported
by the cooler

no i aint never noticed that bafore en probly
cause it aint true but i wasted enough time
arguin with you tanight   i just come out here
tryin ta get a little breeze but i guess the only
thing movin out heres your lips   to bad this aint
a sailboat cause we wouldnt never be lost
for wind

the cuban laughs

how long you thin we gonna have humidity capn

till fall comes i guess   its been late comin so it
aint gonna let go that easy

the captain walks over to the cuban who is sitting on the
gunwale with his legs over the side and a fishing pole in
his hands   in the soft moonlight the line is visible at

the tip of the pole but disappears before it enters the water   the cuban is naked except for a pair of boxer shorts with contrasting stripes that are visible in the dark as black and gray and black and gray   his thick neck spreads to his shoulders that turn into powerful arms that hold the hands that hold the fishing pole before his crotch

> whatre you fishin for there man   you aint playin that line at all   and whatre you usin fer bait   we didn't bring nothin with us this trip cause we aint fishin

> **i not fishin for nutn capn   i jus like to have the pole in my hand**

the cuban plays with the line a little

> **i jus got a little piece of sandich on the hook**

> *maybe he find daht rare fish daht like ham and cheese   i tink i heard of daht fish before*

> a piece a sandwich   well dont this beat all   you done some pretty stupid things with me but damn if this dont top em all

the cuban moves the pole up and down

the captain rubs his hand across his beard

the haitian shifts onto his side so he can see the outline of
the two men better

    cahptane

the captain turns

    well waddaya spect me ta do   call him a genius
       out here fishin almost naked with a sandwich
    on a hook   jesus   besides i always callin you
    stupid too

    no you don capn   you callin him crazy and stuff
    but you not callin him stupid   only me

the captain takes a deep breath

the cuban looks at the haitian and then the captain and
smiles

    it okay capn   i been told i stupid all my life
      i don mine cuz people forgive me cuz of it
      i do somethin wrong and they forgive it   i do
    somethin right and they happy   i don mine capn

the stars are hazy dots in the milky sky and the moon is a
patch of light searching for definition

the haitian rolls onto his back and tucks his hands behind
his head as the cuban continues to raise and lower the
pole   the captain wipes the back of his neck and passes
his mouth across a hairy shoulder and then hitches the
wet pants up to his navel

```
see see    i told daht man he full
of shit    come out here and see
dis cahptane    i told daht man he
full of shit all deh time and now
you can see
```

the captain comes out of the cabin and stands next to the
haitian   they watch the cuban dangling over the side of
the boat crouched in the collapsible outdoor john they
use at sea when they are idle and the weather is calm
the toilet is built of leather and rope and wooden slats
and when not in use hangs flat against the boat from the
lifeline   the device is comfortable and efficient and put
together in such a way that it is a piece of art   it is a
relief from the heavy smells of the head and even the
captain has been known to sit on it reading the paper and
feeding the sea with his spoor

the cuban has a huge smile on his face and his feet are
pressed against the gunwale   he sits easily in the
contraption with his big knees rising to his chin and his
hands holding onto the ropes that hold him to the boat

more feces drop into the water

> dis man shit so bad he killing deh
> fish cahptane   look at dis
> here   daht man is killing
> deh fish

the captain looks over the side   a fish floats on the
surface with dull coated eyes and its mouth open in
legacy of its final gasp for air   the captains blue eyes
scan the ocean in all directions but see no sign of human
beings or any craft

> by jesus he is killin the fuckin fish   what the
> hells in that shit a his   it aint from the food i
> give im

the captain looks up at the cuban

> you got to lay off all that spicy stuff   have that
> woman a yers start cookin a good irish stew or
> some corned beef en cabbage   en do it quick
> man or youll be killin all the fish in the damn
> ocean en we wont have no job no more

wind dancing

the cuban laughs so hard he finds it difficult to catch his
breath and the toilet shakes causing him to hang on
tighter   he finally controls himself and then a stream
of urine falls to the ocean and the laughing begins again

i never bothrn you two when you shitn

   thats cause we aint killin the fish   we got ta
   protect our jobs here man i dont mind ya shittin
   outdoors   in fact i prefer it   but you cant be
   killin all the creatures in the sea

they all laugh

the sun has been peering over the horizon and with the
sound of laughter lifts itself out of the water and pushes
its light across the sea drenching the three men in white
and gold rays   off to the west a gull has appeared and
searches the sky in an endless circular pattern

a wave rolls under the boat making the cuban grab onto
the sides of the toilet and causing the haitian to place his
hand on the captains broad shoulder

hand me that wrench over there

the captain points with a fat tanned finger   he looks for a
rag on the engines and then on the deck and finally gives
up his search and wipes his hands on his pants   he tucks
in half his shirttail and rolls the sleeves of his ragged blue
shirt up his massive forearms

here you go capn

the captain takes the wrench without looking back and
sticks his head into the engine compartment   the cuban
stands and watches while the haitian sets the pince nez
on his nose and leans over the engines with a finger to his
cheek   reaching deep into the black core of the boat the
captain works the wrench with a series of jerking
motions so violent he has to straighten his cap several

times   he wipes his mouth across his shoulder and takes a deep breath before giving one more vicious turn that rips the skin from his knuckles making him drop the wrench into the bilge   his curses echo in the trapped compartment

the cuban covers his mouth

the haitian adjusts the pince nez

retrieving the tool the captain raises himself up with a hand on his back and his lips tight with pain   he wipes a forearm across his eyes   leaning against the engine hatch he wraps a dirty bandana around his knuckles before handing the wrench to the cuban

> i cant tell if its a leak or just a little water down there   take a look wouldya man en make sure that valves shut tight

the cuban places a leg in the engine compartment and lies across the deck   with one hand he works the wrench up and down and up and down and the thick muscles ripple across his back as if small creatures move under his skin   when his hand jerks to a halt and the valve will go no farther he stands and faces the captain

i don think it leakin capn   jus a little water

wind dancing

the captain nods and closes the engine hatch   he
replaces his cap and walks the deck fore and aft before
leaning first over the port side and then over the
starboard side

everthin okay

everything okay capn

you sure there aint nothin over the side

nutn but tha shitter got me in trouble earlier

the captain walks up the short ladder to the bridge and
the silence is shattered as the first diesel roars to life   he
guns the engine sending a ball of blue smoke out the
transom and starts the other engine exhaling another
malignant cloud that agitates the water astern   the boat
vibrates with energy and moves slowly to port while the
captain taps each gauge and checks his heading   he
looks around one more time and gives an awkward wave
to his crew that stand watching him from the transom

the haitian returns the wave and smiles and leans toward
the cuban

daht one happy man now   he always
happy when he get his engines loud
and start moving deh boat

the captain holds the helm with one hand and with the other engages the engines pulling the boat out of its doldrums and moving it through the sea   as the wind increases he removes his greek fishermans cap and places it next to the compass in front of him   he runs a hand over his head and checks all the gauges and then throws a glance across the stern before going to full throttle

the haitian returns to his mattress and puts the pince nez back on his nose and sets off to another sea in another time   his eyes grow wide and his face changes expression as the story moves closer to its climax and the tension builds   he crosses his feet and adjusts his pillow of rags as the pages flutter against his dark hands

the cuban folds a large oil stained rag into a square slightly larger than his hand and begins to wipe the engine hatch   his arm moves in a tight circular motion as he goes over and over each spot and is forced to stand and straighten himself every so often to escape the awkward position he works in

in full stride now the boats wake is a huge v that could be a path back home if it wasnt already fading from sight

a gull flies past in the opposite direction

the cuban moves on to unconquered territory   he wipes the gunwale as the wind paints his face random spray is thrown onto his body and the rising sun massages his

neck   he works his way to the port side of the
superstructure and runs the rag across spots that are real
and imagined   when he reaches the bow he stops his
work and looks at the sea   he places the rag in his back
pocket and walks onto the bowsprit   the wind runs
through the tight hairs on his head and streams across his
chest billowing his shirt into a parachute of red   he
closes his eyes and moves his body from side to side with
a slight bend in his legs   his arms rise slowly over his
head and his smile breaks into a song without words   he
hums and sways and drinks deeply the rich sea salt that
the wind carries in its wake

i feel i dancin capn   i dancin with a wind

the captain checks his compass and looks at the cubans
swaying form and runs a hand over his head

whats that yer sayin man

but the cuban cannot hear and continues his slow
hypnotic dance until the boat chops into a wave and he is
forced to grab onto the lifeline to save his balance   he
smiles and removes the rag from his pocket as he steps off
the bowsprit and renews his cleaning this time down the
starboard side

a small gathering of dolphins follow the boat   they leap
into the air and sink into the sea playing some unknown

game with the boats wake until some internal force tells
them the game is over and they vanish into the dark

the islands comin up   get ready with the
bow line

the cuban strides to the bow and ties one end of the line
to a cleat   he stands and pulls on the rope to make sure
its secure then loops the remaining line into his callused
palm   when finished he stands on the bowsprit his dark
eyes squinting into the sun watching the tiny oval of land
move toward him   the boat strikes a mound of water
shifting the hull to port and sending a light spray over the
bow   the cuban wipes his face with the tail of his shirt
and smiles and waves at the captain

the captain slows the boat and checks his gauges and
looks aft and then forward and brings the engines down
even farther

*it is good to see our little island
again is it not cahptane*

the captain stares straight ahead

go on up there in case our man needs a hand

the haitian moves to the bow and nods to the cuban who
looks at the captain and then at the island

the engines go silent leaving an empty pocket of air that
is soon filled by whispering sand as the boat glides onto
the beach nestling itself against the oasis in the sea   the
cuban coils his body and then swings it gracefully toward
the island releasing the line into the windless humid
air   the rope drifts silently through the blue sky until it
touches the shore creating a strange boundary that runs
from the island to the boat cutting the world in two   the
cuban leaps into the warm sea and raises his arms chest
high as he plods through the clear water watching his
distorted legs take each step   emerging onto dry
land he reaches down and grabs the rope and pulls
toward the lone tree on the island   he takes a turn
around the mutilated black trunk and leans back with his
body chafing the line several inches around the tree   the
cuban stands straight and looks at the boat and then
leans back again   when he gets only half an inch more
he knows the boat is secure and ties off with a series of
half hitches

wind dancing

the captain struggles to shore with a cooler and sets it
down between two disfigured poles of driftwood that
touch ends to form a v   the island is no more than forty
yards by fifteen yards and because of its placement in
the stream catches shells by the thousands on its
western shore   it seems a miracle the tiny spit of land
still exists above water with the constant battering it
receives from nature and the more recent intrusion of
men whose footsteps depress its sand and whose
vagaries alter its content   the island is humped in the
center and covered by rough grass and thin prickly vines
and one ebony palm scarred from lightning or arson
with a single blackened frond hanging limp and
useless   the tree sits a stripped unlit beacon signaling
to no one

the captain shades his eyes with a hand and looks out at
the endless blue and then tips his cap down

making his way onto the beach the haitian hands the
cuban his panama   he wears no hat himself but instead
has replaced the pince nez with a pair of aviator
sunglasses

   heres our movie star   mr hollywood

   *i should know better den to say
   someting like daht to you*

makes me look like a movie stars what you

said   boy if you could see yerself from where i sit
youd know why i cant let that one pass

the haitian walks several paces away and stands in water
to his ankles looking out at the sea with his hands on his
hips   his skin is deep black and his short wiry hair
retreats from his forehead with a brush of gray on the
sides   his legs are bowed with large balls of hard flesh
that are calves and the leg bones traced by thick black
skin   his chest narrows as it rises to his shoulders and is
covered by tight muscles   the exposed ribs make him
look forever underfed and his bony shoulders slope
forward as though he carries his burden before him
small crooked fingers hang from the long rods of muscle
that are his arms and reach almost to his knees   he is
made of spare parts   thats what he has been told and it
makes him laugh because looking in a mirror he can
believe it   but he has always surprised people with his
strength

walking back toward the cooler the haitian shuffles his
wide feet in the water disturbing the sand into clouds of
brown   colonies of tiny fish swim before him going
steadily one way and then in an instant flash off in
another direction

what time is deh pickup tonight
cahptane

midnight

daht is later den usual is it not

i think that mans playin with our heads   but it
dont matter cause we get paid all the same

the captain takes a bite of his sandwich and chews until
there is room for beer

he aint kiddin me with that phony accent a his
either   he aint no more haitian then i am   but
let him play his games cause i think its time ta up
the price for the next pickup

the haitian rolls a can of coke between his palms

> *i am surprised to hear you talk of*
> *anudder pickup cahptane   usually*
> *it is always dis is deh last one*
> *dis is deh last one aint no more*
> *of deze pickups for me*

the cuban laughs

the captain takes a sip of beer   he tucks the meat back
under the bread of his sandwich and then wipes his
fingers on his pants

> well maybe i do but not this time   we need a
> fair price for the risk we take en i aim ta get it

> *he will just raise deh price for deh*
> *people cahptane   dey are poor and*
> *cannot afford what dey pay already*

> that aint none a my concern   we got ta get paid a
> fair price en how he gets the money aint no
> bother ta me   this whole deals not gonna last
> forever en i keep hearin theyre gonna increase
> patrols off the key

the captain looks up at the sun and then out to sea

we cant be doin this too often or the coast guardll
catch on for sure   thats why we gotta get more
for each run

a wave washes onto the island cleansing the beach with a
film of white foam before noiselessly retreating into the
sea discarding shells and seaweed and a bleached piece
of wood that struggles to follow but becomes helplessly
trapped in the sand

*couldnt we take more people on
deh boat*

the captain runs the back of his hand across his mouth

we ride damm low as it is   we aint taken one
more body on this boat en thats the end a that

the haitian removes his sunglasses and wipes his face on
the tail of his oversized shirt   he stares at the cooler as he
rubs the lenses and then checks his work against the sun
before placing them over his eyes

*its just daht dey are so poor
cahptane*

the men eat and sweat under the yellow sun   a light
breeze offers little relief from the heat but keeps the bugs

away so there are no complaints only silent resignation to the world as it stands

a gull lands on the disfigured palm and faces into the breeze   it spreads its wings and hops up and down several times as if to take flight but chooses instead to remain perched on its pedestal   it stares down at the three men who sit on the driftwood with the cooler between them and twitches its head perhaps trying to comprehend their noise   then the gull opens its mouth as if yawning   spreads it wings and with a single push flies away

capn   come here capn   quick

the captain and the haitian look at each other   the
captain shakes his head and stands

now whats that man got himself inta

*maybe he catch a fish wit some of
his sandwich*

the haitian rises and sees the cuban standing on the other
side of the island waving his large hands   he adjusts his
glasses as he follows the captain shuffling his feet through
the water and looking for any remarkable shells   they
round the southern tip of the island and come to the
cuban who stands erect wringing his hands and shifting
his weight from one foot to the other   beside him is a

small hole where the sand has been dug away   from
within the hole a small object points at the sky

    ya look like ya done somethin wrong ens waitin
    for the teacher ta holler

**i done nutn capn   i step on something an i look
down and think maybe it a shell so i dig a little
it no shell capn**

the captain and the haitian look into the hole   a tiny
broken digit is tilted toward the sun   its tip has been
gnawed to a bleached bone surrounded by pink flesh
freckled with sand and swollen to bursting   tiny
knuckles resembling arranged stones or the vertebrae of
some insignificant creature push gently out of the
earth   tiny white worms scurry for darkness

    sweet fuckin jesus whatve ya come by man

the captain kneels down and tilts his head to one side to
inspect the finger   he stares at it a moment without a word
then he cups his hands in front of the object and in a slow
easy motion pulls the sand toward his body careful not to
touch the rotting flesh and piling the earth against his knees
   a minute fist is uncovered   its fingers are folded tightly into
its palm as though grasping for something except for the one
chewed appendage that points accusingly toward the sky

the captain places his palms on his thighs and stares at
the hand rising from the dark defiled sand with its angry
dead skin withering under the sun   he exhales loudly
and wipes his open shirt across his face looking at the dirt
that has come from his body before tucking the tail back
in his pants   he stares out at the still ocean   he wipes a
forearm across his forehead   he bends over and digs
deeper revealing first a wrist and then an arm and then a
small shoulder   as his hands reenter the earth once
more a foul pocket of air releases an overwhelming
stench that makes the captain sit back on his heels and
gag for unpolluted air

he rests

he plunges his hands again into the damp earth

the cuban and the haitian stand dumb   they watch as
first a shoulder and then the neck and then the head of
the baby are released from the soil

the sun plays its light on the exhumed sand

a gull circles overhead and disappears

the captain continues to dig

    christ another

a right hand appears with the tiny fingers in the same strange fisted pointer as the first only the black skin is a testimonial to the buriers lack of prejudice

the captain cleans the head of a child   the eyeless face stares at him looking old and tired with its withered skin and flattened ears and the tiny mouth that struggled for air   the captains sweat drops into the cavity of ruin scattering the maggots and washing spots of dirt from the flesh   he digs away at the second hand trying to find another head but instead comes to more maggots and another hand

water rises slowly into the hole

the captain stands and looks at his palms   without a word he walks waist deep into the sea and holds his hands under water as he turns his head to the island

sickest damn thing i ever saw

the cuban walks into the sea

what we gonna do capn

the captain returns to shore with the cuban in his wake and looks down into the hole

nothin

the haitian looks at him and then at the destroyed
children

```
we have to do someting cahptane
we cannot just leave dem here
dehr may be    i dont know
cahptane    dehr may be ten or
twenty of deze babies hidden in deh
ground
```

the men stand looking at the uncovered death

    we aint sayin nothin

the captain pushes sand back over the exposed flesh with
his foot

```
cahptane    we must tell deh
atorities    maybe we can notify
deh coast guard    deh men daht did
dis cannot get away
```

they already have gotten away   what do we do
then   call the coast guard en tell im we was out here
fishin en stumbled on this island   in case ya fergot
we snuck out in the middle a the night en we aint
had the radio on at all   thered be too many questions
en we aint got enough good answers ta go around

he moves the last of the sand into place but the one finger is still visible above ground   the captain places his foot down on the mutilated flesh and presses it into the sand

by christ its a sick fuckin world we walk on taday

he pushes additional sand into the depression and packs it down with both feet

we must tell someone cahptane

tell yerself en keep it at that   aint nothin anyone can do for these poor souls now   en we still got a job ta do

the cuban stares at the trampled earth

who could do this capn   who could kill babies

the humidity weighs the men down as they return to the other side of the island and prepare to board the boat they work under the fiery sun in silence except for the sound of the ocean as wave after wave tumbles onto the sand finally relieved of its interminable journey   a few emaciated clouds stretch across the western sky offering no shade or hope only a vague contrast to the endless

wind dancing

blue   and sightless maggots return to their gruesome task
without pleasure or pain

the captain takes the cooler   the haitian carries a plastic
bag with their trash and the cuban unties the bow line
from the dying tree and wades through the warm sea to
the boat

returning to the island the gull lands on the matted sand
among the captains footprints   the bird stands facing
the wind and aims its beak at the earth as if to peck at
something but instead lifts suddenly into the air   it
circles the island once and then twice before settling
onto the beleaguered palm to witness the boat and its
crew disappear into the southern horizon

hand me another beer there wouldya

the cuban reaches into the cooler and removes a beer and
hands it to the captain

won be long now will it capn

the captain raises his arm and his watch catches the
moons light

we still got plenty a time

the boat sways gently back and forth

sweat glides down the captains face   he takes a drink
before pressing the can to his forehead and rolling it side
to side while his other hand pulls the front of his soaked
shirt from his body

the haitian pulls the bottom of his tee shirt out of his
pants and wipes his face

```
dis night keeps getting wetter and
wetter    like its raining witout
deh rain
```

i cant hardly breathe   its like i gotta work ta keep
the air goin in en outa my lungs

the captain tips his head forward rivers of sweat roll down
his neck and hide in the forest of hairs on his chest   he
finishes the beer and tosses the can into the open plastic bag
on deck and wipes the back of his hand across his mouth

toss me another one

the cuban lifts a can from the cooler and pitches it to the
captain

gonna be good when we get this boat movin

stripped to a pair of cutoff shorts and a smile the cuban
wipes his chest with a towel already damp with sweat

the moons diffused light drops puddles of white into the
black sea   the stars are obscure as though the universe is
searching for proper focus and only the occasional sound

of breaking water occupies the night when the men are
silent

> *it is like we are out in deh middle*
> *of space tonight   like we are not*
> *even on deh eart*

oh christ but i knew youd start gettin
philasophical on me   i need somethin substantial
ta listen ta this

the captain disappears into the cabin and returns
squeezing the neck of a bottle   he sits on the gunwale
and places the whiskey between his heavy legs   with
one hand he liberates the cap and tosses it into the
sea   he presses the bottle to his lips and takes two long
drinks before chasing it with a draft of beer

the cuban looks at the haitian but in the fragile light
cannot see his expression

you wanna coke capn

a coke   christ but i dont know bout you
sometimes man   i got a beer in my hand en a
bottle a decent whiskey between my legs   i aint
exactly at a loss fer somethin ta drink right now
ya drink all the coke ya want   but i need

somethin ta take the edge off when i listen ta mister philasopher here

the haitian tilts his head as he looks at the captain

> *why are you drinking so much*
> *tonight cahptane   most of deh*
> *time you are very careful to be*
> *sober on deh night of a pickup*

the captain takes another sip of whiskey before setting it against his soaked crotch   he rubs one bare foot over the other

> i can handle my liquor dont you worry   i aint
> drunk en i wont be when the time comes   en
> maybe yer the reason i need a good stiff one
> tanight

> *i will not philosophise any more*
> *cahptane*

> it aint yer fancy talkin   its you en yer fuckin
> questions that sets me on edge   am i married
>   do i have a woman   its like gettin the third
> degree en i aint done nothin wrong but maybe
> give ya a job that puts food on the table en
> clothes on yer back   en lets ya buy all those
> books ya read   maybe all those books is the

problem   puttin all these crazy questions in yer
head that you aint got the sense ta keep ta
yerself   i aint gotta explain nothin ta you

i just aint marrieds all

the cuban shuffles items around in the cooler and hums
a song

i aint gotta explain nothin ta no one

the captain picks up his bottle and walks to the bow   he
sits on the deck and looks out over the shadowy sea as he
breaths deeply and rolls his head from side to side   he
finishes the beer and tosses it into the black mouth of the
ocean

*i tought you did not want us to
trow anyting over deh side*

the captain jerks his head around to the haitian   his face
tightens as if he will scream but instead looks over the
bow and takes a drink

aint no one gonna know its us threw that can a
beer in the drink   besides   itll be at the
bottom a the ocean soon enough

*i did not mean to upset you wit my
questions cahptane*

bullshit   you always tryin ta get under my skin
only this time ya done it too good

*i am just curious as to why you do
not have a woman is all*

curiosity killed the cat there man   ya might be
smart ta ramember that

the captain tilts the bottle to his lips and then places it
between his knees and wipes his mouth with his hand

i aint got no wife en never will   theres a whore i
been seein for almost ten year now   i met her at a
party of another captain she come on ta me like
lightnin en i thought she was married ta that
captain en i tell ya i didnt know what ta do   but
she got ta me so we went back ta her place en
when its all over i finally find out she aint nobodys
bride by a long shot   we got us some laughs outa
that alright   anyway she aint whorin like she used
ta   just a couple a us old timers shes known for
years   seein her once in a whiles all i need

the cubans singing floats up from the stern

wind dancing

i remember one time fallin asleep at her place
we had us a time that night en i just passed right
out   not too drunk or nothin   we just had us a
hell of a time

just deh one time you slept dehr

christ yes man   when i woke up i never felt so
good as to be restin against those big titties a
hers   but when i come ta realize what i done en
where i was i jumped up en dressed en was outa
there fast

the haitian leans forward and rubs his calves

*why dont you like to stay wit her
cahptane*

the captain drinks more whiskey   the alcohol rolls down
his chin and falls unimpeded onto his lap

you en yer fuckin questions

he drinks again and looks at the half empty bottle

cause i aint gonna thats all   ever mans gotta see
what he is   gotta know what kinda stock he
comes from en whats inside him en take that inta

71

account all his life   thats why i aint stayed
with her

he lets out a deep breath as sweat pours from his face

fuckin humiditys gonna kill us tonight

the boat rolls across a black swell of sea

the captain bestows a long kiss to the open end of the
bottle

ya gotta know who ya are en where ya come from

and who are you cahptane

me   i come from a dirty man   a real dirty man

the captain takes his cap off and wipes at the sweat on his
head   then replaces the cap and drinks again

i used ta worship my father   he was a tough son
of a bitch but i still used ta think he was all a man
could be   en i got in a fight one night   by
christ i got in a fight one night with my best
friend   at fourteen who doesnt fight with their
friends   i was stayin at his house that night
but we got in a scuffle en i bloodied his nose so
that was the end a that night en i went home   i

wind dancing

went home en i shouldnta   i shoulda done
anythin else

the whiskey pours into his body and the sweat pours out
and the moon becomes ever more hazy behind the wall
of humidity

    i come up ta the door a the house en i stop cause i
    hear a noise   so i go ta the kitchen windah en
    take a look   en then i come ta see whats the stuff
    that makes me   my poor sister aint but sixteen
    ens leanin on the counter ens got her dress on her
    back en panties around her ankles en her mouth
    is ugly a sight as i ever seen cause her lips are all
    red en kinda in a square like there shoulda been a
    scream comin out   but there aint nothin but a
    deep throaty noise comin out ever so often   en
    behind hers my father   my fuckin father with
    his pants down en his hard on ploughin inta my
    sister en a look a the devil on his face

    cahptane

    whats a matter   all of a sudden ya wish ya aint
    asked no questions   well too late now   ya asked
    en i told ya   i sat outside that windah en listened
    till the old mans done en finally raised his
    pants   he heads out the door en never even seen
    me en heads to the bar or the boat or i dont know

where   en all a time i lie under the windah en
dont wanna get up cause i dont want my sister ta
know i seen her   en then i hear my mothers
voice   christ but what a family this is huh
sheed been in the other room all a time   she
made little cooing sounds en i look up en shes
holdin my sisters head in her shoulder en pattin
her back   well thats it for me i knew right
then   my mother en sister go up stairs for a
while i guess ta clean up my sister en then they
come out the front door en i watch em go down
that street real slow   when theyre outa sight i
grab all the stuff i can carry en i get outa there
fast en head south

the captain turns to the haitian

so thats why i aint gettin married   cause whats
in yer fathers in you   en lookit the whole
family   my father a damn freak en my mother
goin along with it although i guess she didnt like
it none   still she coulda taken a knife ta the old
man en put a end to it

the boat rolls

the captain drinks

en me   i just watched   i coulda run in en

grabbed a knife myself or just pummel the dirty
bastard with my fists   but i watched en then slid
ta the ground with these big tears rollin down my
face   so anyway thats whats in me en i aint
puttin no kids through that   no sir i aint puttin
no kids through that

the captain finishes the bottle and tosses it into the sea

the haitian wipes his face with the front of his shirt

water breaks off the starboard bow sending lines of
wavering white across the ocean

toss down the goods

the skipper of the refugee boat looks down at the captain

YOU SURE YOU DONT WANT TO DO THIS FOR
FREE OLD MAN

toss down the damn money or i leave ya with yer
stinkin load

the captain of the refugee ship tosses a small canvas bag
onto the deck of the boat

pull away there man

the cuban engages the engines and steers the boat away
from the ship in a wide arc   the diesels broken voice
reverberates through the midnight sky and the boats

wake churns the water to cotton dissolving the moons
reflection

lifting his cap the captain runs a forearm over his eyes
he stares at the dark outline of the haitian and scratches
at his beard as his body sways to the rhythm of spirits
coursing through his veins

    youll be gettin yer people soon enough   soon as i
    make sure the moneys all there

the ocean lifts the bow of the boat and shoulders its way
along the hull until it reaches the stern where it tips the
captains body forward   he reaches for the gunwale but
it eludes his grasp pitching him into an absurd dance
until his hands catch the deck and the greek fishermans
cap slides to a blackened corner of the boat   crouching
on all fours the captain struggles for air

    just let me get my money   my fuckin moneys all
    i want

a small stream of saliva hangs from his lower lip a
moment before detaching itself and dropping onto
the deck

    capn   capn

the captain hauls himself erect   he feels the top of his
head with one hand and looks at the distance the cuban
has set between the two vessels   his other hand grasps
the gunwale

okay   thats good right there man

the cuban takes the boat out of gear and the diesels cough
several times before settling into a murmur

with exaggerated care the captain retrieves the canvas
bag and leans against the engine hatch   he reaches
inside and seizes a banded stack of currency that he
weighs in his palm before raising it up to what little light
the night provides   he turns the bills in one direction
and his head in another but the denominations remain
veiled by a fragile moon and anesthetized eyes   the old
man curses as sweat runs off his thick wrists fathering
dark circular spots that turn the bills soft   he exhales
audibly through bloated cheeks and rubs a thumb across
the money   he gulps for air several times and then his
body jerks as a sour belch rises to his lips   he spits onto
the deck and moves a hand across his mouth and then
across his pants but never removes his gaze from the bag

overhead the moon struggles for recognition as the night
grows sodden and heavy and black clouds cover what
remains of the stars to the south

the boat slowly rotates in the sea until its starboard side
faces the refugee ships port side   the two vessels now
mimic prize fighters searching for weaknesses or perhaps
cowards preparing to bolt in different directions

the haitian looks at the refugee ship that holds his people and
can still smell the urine and feces and vomit that assaulted
him as the boats passed each other   he tries to pick out faces
he may know through the diffused moonlight but confronts
only the outline of the ship with patches of flesh lining the
gunwale   with his hands in fists and a quivering muscle in
his jaw the haitian stares at the ship through watery eyes

> *i miss you woomahn   i miss you*
> *too much*

he places a hand on his pocket and lightly touches the
outline of the pince nez

standing on the bridge the cuban watches the movements
of the men below   then he turns and glances at the bow
before checking the gauges and setting the wheel
amidships   softly humming he makes his way down to
the deck

the captain replaces the money in the bag and heads
down into the cabin   doors open and slam shut and
curses drift up to the night where they dissolve in the
humidity   at last he returns on deck wiping his bare

head with a bandanna and the handle of a pistol sticking
out of his wet pants

    its all there   give em the signal

the haitian looks at the gun

   cahptane   dis is a bad night to
   have deh gun out   dehr will be no
   trouble witout deh gun

   give em the signal en shut up

the haitian retrieves a large flashlight from a
compartment at the stern   he turns it on and waves
it back and forth at the ship   its fragile arc of white
disturbs a small portion of the night   and then
goes dark

no birds circle overhead   no dolphins play in the
sea   nothing surfaces to feed   there are only two ships
rolling across the sea under a wounded moon and absent
stars

concerned that they have not seen his light the haitian
raises the flashlight to give the signal one more time but
before he can release the beacon a body falls from the
refugee ship   a single tear of humanity is wept into the
black sea

the diesels murmur and the heat veils the stars and the
fluctuating moonlight falls on the head of a man moving
unevenly toward the boat   he rises and falls to some
foreign rhythm as his arms and legs work forward and his
face lifts to sample the air and then dips back into the sea
to taste death for a instant before spitting it back into the
night

there is another splash

and another

the ship disgorges its contents into the sea

the solemn heads of midnight swimmers bob through the
ocean

and still another splash

and another

wind dancing

a swimmer nears the boat   one hand paddles him
unevenly forward as the other hand holds a small plastic
suitcase above his head   raised out of the water is the
material sum of existence among the poor   memories in
cardboard and plastic and tin

the swimmers hand touches the boat and the haitian
reaches down and helps him on board   the man stands
in a ragged pair of shorts and smiles at the outlines of the
crew as the sea falls from his body   the haitian speaks to
him in french and points to the bow   the man shakes
the haitians hand and takes his grin past the captain and
the cuban and sits behind the bowsprit wrapping his
arms around the leaking suitcase and staring toward
what he hopes is a new home

another swimmer climbs aboard   a frail old man with
no plastic suitcase and no smile   he bows slightly from
the waist but does not shake hands and without a word
works his way forward to where the first man sits

```
dey coming now cahptane     dey
coming on board and will see
freedom soon
```

the swimmers continue to climb out of the water and be
helped by the haitian who speaks to them in soothing
tones and directs them to their place on the boat

the captain leans against the engine hatch and
wipes his head with the soaked bandanna and soon
counts what should be the last refugee to come
aboard

but still they swim to the boat

and in the distance still they drop into the sea

> hey hey   whats this here now   thats the last one
> on board this boat

the captain cups his hands and aims his mouth at the
refugee ship

> we got our load   stop em from goin inta the
> water wouldja man   stop em now

there is no response

the captain turns to the haitian

> dont let no more come on board   stop em right
> there

> *but cahptane   we cannot leave
> dem here*

wind dancing

stop em en send em back   unless they got
money on em ta pay   then i might think about
it   otherwise they go back

i cannot cahptane

ya will en ya better

the haitian calls in french to the swimmers and sweeps
an arm toward the boat

a man touches the transom   the haitian helps him to the
deck and directs him forward but the captain catches the
man by his shoulders

ya got any money man

the captain shakes him violently

ya got any money i say

the haitian and the man speak

*he has no money cahptane   he gave
everyting to deh cahptane of
daht ship*

the captain lifts the poor creature from his feet and tosses
him into the sea

cahptane   you cannot cahptane
dey need help

the haitian looks out to the sea and calls the man back to the boat

yer the one needs help

the haitian turns and stares at the gun leveled at his chest

the captain wipes his head with the bandanna

the cuban is frozen

dey need our help cahptane   dey
need our help   dey will be no
trouble   see

he points to the men already on the boat and then turns and urges the swimmers forward

he looks back at the captain

we already left doze babies
behind   do we leave everyting
behind us cahptane   do we not try
to help anyone   dey are my
people   dey will be no trouble
dey are my people

and the explosion from the gun hurls the haitians body
over the side and into the sea leaving a small stream of
blood in the night

no capn

the cuban grabs the captain   the gun falls to the deck

no

and the captain is turned and pounded against the
bulkhead

a neck snaps

a head drops to a chest

a body slides to the deck and leans against the gunwale

the cuban backs several steps away   he looks at his
hands and at the silent men about the deck and then at
the black form hunched over with its bald head reflecting
a distant light and its open eyes drinking death   he
backs away one more step and his foot touches the
gun   gently he taps his foot on the deck until he places
the toe of his sandal on the pistol trapping it to the
boat   then with all eyes watching he picks up the gun
and places it carefully into the sea

and on the other side of the night the refugee ship

engages its engines and moves off into space leaving a trail of bodies treading the sea

the cuban watches the ship until its black form is long past his eyes   he breathes deeply letting the salt attack his head and the air inflate his lungs and then exhales looking at the heads dotting the water   he looks over at the body

   i in it now capn   i in it deep

the men on the boat stare at him as he wipes the sweat from his face and leans over the transom

   come on   come on   get on a boat

he waves his hand and the swimmers once again swim to the boat

and each body that climbs on board shakes the cubans hand and moves silently to an empty space

and each body that climbs on board settles the boat a little lower into the sea

when at last the ocean is empty the cuban looks around at his cargo and then out at the darkness   he runs his eyes from the waterline of the boat to where the night swallows the sea but the haitians body is nowhere to be seen

wind dancing

he looks back at his ragged cargo

we gotta go

he looks for someone who understands

**the gun made a big noise   i don know how far it
wen   that why the ship wen away   i don know
who else out here   we gotta go**

he steps around the bodies and climbs to the bridge and
starts the boat moving into the night

the sky too thick   i ken see nutn

a heavy fog presses against the earth and the sea is a sheet
of gray that wavers with each passing swell   the sound of
the diesels is muffled and comforting and holds the mist
and the ocean together with its voice

the cuban slows the boat to a touch more than idle   the
vessel crawls tentatively forward as if on all fours and the
diesels cough and hack a blue black cloud from the
transom protesting the torpid pace

leaving the helm the cuban weaves his way around the
squatting bodies to find a free spot on the bow so he can
speak to his crew

you gotta look for stuff in a water   you gotta
lookout

he holds a hand over his eyes as if shading them from the sun and stretches his neck toward the sea while his head runs dramatically from one side of the ocean to the other   the men nod in unison and smile and stand at the lifeline looking into the fog

that it   that it   you gotta look out for stuff in a water   okay   look out for stuff in a water

the cuban returns to the bridge and sets the boat back on course   one large hand rests easily on the helm and the other wipes the mist from his forehead and hair and the back of his neck

i gotta go slow right capn   i go slow an take it easy an keep my course cuz they not no wind to blow us too far away

he watches his lookouts

i gotta go slow

the ragged men scan the few feet they can see although it seems only inches because the fog and sea are all the same color in the early morning light   they speak no word but look intently into the colorless planet with the rags hanging off their bodies and their skin covered with sweat and mist   the reverberating diesels seem to own the worlds voice so it is startling when water breaks off

the starboard bow and the noise is amplified to their
ears   they turn and point and speak freely but quietly to
each other

the cuban notices

what is it   what you see

they turn and realize their mistake   a middle aged man
waves his arms and then makes his hand into a fish
jumping out of the water   he smiles

okay   okay   i see

the fog is a thick gray blanket dropped over the boat yet
each tiny drop is so defined it seems they are moving
under a sky of levitating pearls   it is a cool translucent
atmosphere foreign to these tropical latitudes that seems
to have drifted too far south in its sleep

the cuban checks the gauges and the compass and runs a
broad hand over his head and then looks at his lookouts

they okay capn   they gonna do okay

**where the sun capn   the sun gotta come out
some time**

the sky is light gray and indistinguishable from the sea
unless seen against the hull of the ship   the ocean is flat
and unbroken but for a migrant swell and the acrobatics
of certain fish twisting up from the depths   these flying
creatures jump in pursuit or escape and the refugees
have become accustomed to their flight from the sea and
point with their chins toward the sound

occasionally someone urinates over the side or sits
unembarrassed in the portable john that the cuban has
shown them how to use and defecates into the sea   no
one pays attention except the cuban who watches
through the haze and understands what is in their past to
induce such determination

the cuban taps one of the gauges and the needle quivers and then settles back to its original position   he takes a deep breath and runs his shirttail over his eyes and mouth

we gotta eat capn   we gotta eat somethin

he motions for a boy in his early teens to come up to the bridge   the young man rises and staggers to the cuban with his eyes wide

you gotta steer a boat   okay   here   put your hands on a helm

he guides the teens hands to the wheel

don steer too much

he turns the wheel vigorously back and forth   the teen laughs   the cuban looks at him full in the face and shakes his handsome head back and forth

no   no   is no good to do like tha   no good

he holds the delicate hands steady and points a finger to the compass

keep it there   jus like that

the teen nods and stands as though made of brick with
arms of concrete glued to the wheel

relax   you gonna relax   okay

the cuban climbs down to the deck and enters the cabin
and returns after a time with the cooler   the refugees
make room and peer over his shoulder as he opens the lid

he tears the sandwiches into bite size pieces and hands
the food to one set of hands and they pass it to someone
unseen who passes it on again until the farthest away
receives their meal first and the first will be last to eat
   the ritual is repeated with the bottles of beer passing
from hand to hand   the cuban leans against the
gunwale and dines with his strange guests who now
whisper a little louder

they good people capn   they gonna do okay

the captains head rests against the gunwale and his body
is positioned as if he has fallen asleep from exhaustion

**see   we could take more on board easy   it
was easy**

the cuban wipes his mouth with his shirt   when he has
finished eating he moves to the bridge and is

accompanied by the low sound of many mercis   he
places his hands on the helm and thanks the boy

    go eat   there still some left

the teen looks at him

    go eat   you done good

he places a hand on the young mans shoulder

    bueno

the boy smiles and says bon and moves away to eat

i gotta sleep capn   i ken go no more
i   gotta sleep

the cuban shuts the diesels down and places his arms
around the helm and his head in his arms   his brain is
filled with the sea and fog and black blood squirting into
the night and the sound of delicate bones being snapped
and the feel of it running through his hands and all the
images blurring until finally there is only gray and then
black and then sleep

the displaced sit huddled on deck in different postures of
sleep or semi sleep amidst a tangle of crossed legs and
folded arms   prayerlike hands are tucked between
legs chasing a cold that does not exist   a low song of

steady breathing occupies the sea and is sporadically
broken by the sharp tone of a voice escaping a dream and
painting itself across the black fog   a wet cough raises a
man to his knees long enough to expectorate a bloody
mucus over the side and imagines his wife and child
crying in the night with arms outstretched and rags
hanging from their bodies   he reaches a hand to them
and coughs and soon closes his jaundiced eyes returning
to the fitful sleep that is left to him   another man rises
on the bow exposing himself to the night as he urinates
over the side and rubs a hand over his face and hair
when finished he covers himself and leans against the
lifeline looking out at the surrounding fog   he takes a
small plastic bag from inside his shirt and removes a
crumpled package from which he withdraws a battered
cigarette   miraculously still dry he lights it with a
rusted lighter   he inhales deeply and holds the smoke
in his lungs as long as he can before releasing it through
his nose and mouth   he picks a piece of tobacco from
his lip and flicks it into the sea   each time he inhales
the burning tip crawls toward his face and each time he
exhales the smoke is swallowed by the black night and
when he can smoke no more tosses the butt into the
ocean and returns to the spot on deck that is his

a rolling mound of water tips the boat from side to side
and the twine of arms and legs stretches and untwists
and redistributes into new positions of slumber

wind dancing

the silence now is measureless   absolute   a blanket
of black that deadens the dreams of refugees and
envelops the burning mind of an unwilling captain and
makes the sun seem more precious than ever and ever
more distant

a voice calls into the night

a cough rumbles from a chest

and the captain remains seated in his awkward posture
simulating sleep and denying space to the living

the sky and sea are black and the moon and stars do not
appear and without the occasional surfacing of fish
seldom has the earth been so quiet or so empty

wha   wha   tha you capn

the cuban rubs his eyes and looks at the withered hand
that touches him and then at the face of an old man

whas a matter

the cuban rises from the captains chair   the fog is still
with him but the sun is high enough now to have turned
the earth from black to gray and the bodies on deck from
spirits to homo sapiens

the old man places his hand once again on the cuban and
smiles   he points down to the captain and then turns to
the cuban pinching his nose

the cubans eyebrows press together

the old man waves a hand in front of his nose

the capn   the capn always smell a little   we laugh bout it sometime but we get used to it

the cuban smiles and looks down at the old man

you get used to it

the man bends down and shovels air over his shoulder

the cuban looks

the old man shovels again

ohhh   no   no   you cant put the capn in a water   he don like a water   he try to hide it but i see he don like a water   no   he don like to swim

the old man smiles and pats the cubans solid arm and returns to the deck

the cuban looks at the surrounding fog and rubs his eyes and stares at the lifeless gauges as if they hold the answer to a question that has yet to enter his head   the young man who steered the boat climbs to the bridge and hands him a can of coke and one of the few remaining cookies while in the background the sea parts for a body to enter

thank you   merci

wind dancing

the boy smiles and watches as the cuban starts the diesels
and taps each gauge in turn   the engines roar gives life
to the sea and a sense of purpose to the refugees who
stand and stretch their limbs   the cuban looks at them
and at the empty space next to the cabin and sets the
boat moving forward

thas all there is . there no more

the cuban looks at the men

**i look everywhere   there no more to eat or
drink   accep a little water   we gotta save tha**

the refugees sit back on the deck   their faces blank
their bodies still   prisoners of space and fog
allowed to only sit or stand or coil into a ball and
sleep   a small boy stands at the transom with the
captains cap hiding his eyes and ears   around his
delicate neck is a length of string at the end of which
hang the pince nez   the gold rims are warped and
tarnished and the lenses useless spiderwebs of glass   the
boy pushes the cap up on his head as he moves an
imaginary helm from port to starboard and when he

imitates rising over a wave the brim falls again over his eyes invoking his quiet laughter and a wet cough that shakes his limbs

the cuban also smiles

okay capn   i get back to a wheel   i steer a boat

he salutes the boy and climbs to the bridge and takes the helm from the teenager who remains next to the cuban and looks into the heavy fog   he swirls a near empty bottle of beer in his hand   he offers it to the cuban who smiles and shakes his head no

we gotta get outa this fog

the cuban rubs his face and head and breathes deeply he looks back at the empty faces and the boy who plays captain and then at the teenager   he smiles and glances at the compass before returning his eyes to the fog

i gonna come back to you chica   i gonna come back an hug you an kiss you an take you out to eat anywhere you wanna go   anywhere

the cuban turns and looks at the teenager who stares at the fog

i think of home

wind dancing

but the young man looks straight ahead

and then the cubans hand moves the throttle a fraction
above idle

jus lookout   don move a boat   jus look

the cuban shades his eyes and the teenager nods

climbing down to the deck the cuban walks over to a
group of men who crouch above a trembling body   an
old man inside the circle presses a folded rag to the sick
mans sweltering forehead and then wipes it across the
jaundiced eyes and sunken cheeks before catching a drop
of saliva that drains from the parted lips   the old man
looks up at the cuban and mimics coughing and points at
the sick man who erupts into a coughing fit   the
hacking is violent and broken as though his insides are
coming apart with the pieces tumbling around in his
chest and each spasm contorts the mans face into a mask
of misery   a fountain of spittle erupts from his mouth
the man soils himself

les move him into a cabin

the cuban points to the cabin door   the old man nods
he rises and speaks to the men gesturing first to the
trembling soul on deck and then opening his arms to the
rest of the boat   the men look at the deck   at their
feet   at the cuffs of their tattered pants   they rub their
beards and fold their arms and wash their hands under
imaginary water or roll back what sleeves are left on their
threadbare shirts   and the silence is pure but painful
until a vicious cough explodes from a disintegrating chest
forcing all eyes on the wretched brother who gazes
wildly into the gray mist and whose body trembles for
life   finally four men step forward and lift the sick man
carefully in their arms while keeping their heads turned
away   they look to the old man who signals his
approval before they carry the withering flesh and bone
through a wave of retreating bodies   all watch as the
sick man disappears past the cabin door and then a
mournful silence falls over the refugees   even the boy
tucks himself into a corner by the transom and fingers the
pince nez without a word

a wave rolls under the boat

the engine coughs and spits and fouls the air with blue
smoke

a man stands and tucks his shirt in his ragged pants and
another unties and reties his filthy sneakers and another

picks at his fingernails with a small knife   then someone rises and moves aft   a few words are exchanged and a few gestures given and there is even a brief bit of laughter while everywhere imagined coughs are suppressed and inflamed throats are ignored and hands wipe across foreheads lingering a moment to examine for fever

the cuban and the old man and the four orderlies return on deck

the cuban climbs to the bridge and without a word sets the boat moving through the mist

me   you wan me down there

the cuban points at himself and the old man nods his
head   he gives the helm to the teenager who he now
considers first mate and makes his way down to the deck
past the standing refugees to the starboard side of the
boat   the old man taps the cubans chest and then flaps
his fingers against the thumb of his right hand to mimic
speech

i don know what to say

the old man smiles

the passengers are silent and still

the young boy stands as far away as possible with the cap
in his hand and the pinze nez perched on his nose with
tears running under the crooked rims and down his face

gray fog streams past the mourners and the cuban stares
up at where the sky should be

**the capn believe in god   en tha crazy man with
a glasses didn   i don know if this man believe
or not   but if he did please take him god to
where it safe   an there no more fog**

he looks around

ahmen   okay

the old man touches his arm and signals to the men who
drop the body into the sea and all watch as it glides away
to the south and all feel the boat rise a little higher out of
the water

i getn tired   you better steer a boat

the teenager relieves the cuban of the helm   first he
taps each gauge lightly with his finger and then he steers
the boat to port lining the compass up precisely on
course   he prefers to stand instead of sit by leaning his
small frame against the front of the captains chair with
his bare feet planted wide apart and his hands resting
lightly on the helm

the cuban sits on the bridge and looks down at the deck
and his sad cargo

oh no   not again

on deck another body is carried past the men   past the
empty faces that betray no sentiment and offer no
comforting words to a failed member of this battered

tribe   one man makes the sign of the cross   another
stares at the body from beneath intertwined hands
shading his eyes from an imagined sun   still another
bores his gaze into the deck with one finger tracing
images in immovable sand and his head lying across a
forearm propped between two bony knees   and folding
itself over this procession of death is the vibrating song of
a bloody cough rattling a tiny chest and tearing innocent
eyes as hands play with corroded wire and broken glass
oblivious to the larger world

the body is carried down to the cabin

the sun sinks unnoticed except for the changing color of
mist from gray to black

the men reappear from the cabin minus their load and
return to their spaces on deck   it is the same men who
carried the first sick man   they are now the orderlies
the pallbearers   the symbol for sickness and the symbol
for darkness and are given what little extra space is
available   huddled together they speak only among
themselves while surrounded by the backs of the other
refugees and fog and silence

from his perch on the bridge the cuban watches the
people below   they are hazy images   spirits draped in
gray   as if the present is already the past   already a

memory that he now shares with his wife and children and grandchildren   a memory so real he can feel the vibration of the engines and hear its monotonous snore and taste the gritty exhaust and see each sad face and smell the death that is everywhere

he looks at the mate and then at the men below and then down at the deck between his legs

we gonna get married chica   you right   it time we get married

a tear falls

i don care what a family think   we gonna get married

oh no   oh no

the cuban looks up at the teenager who sits in the
captains chair leaning to one side   his chest
rhythmically rises and falls

oh no   we cant both sleep

the cuban lifts himself to his feet   the compass rotates
to starboard as the boat circles to port

get up

the cuban shakes the young man who rubs his eyes and
looks at the cuban and then at the compass and then
speaks in rapid french

the cuban puts up a hand

is okay   go get some sleep   is okay

they trade places

the teenager stands next to the cuban wanting to be tall
and strong and responsible but his eyes are half closed
and his hair is spiked and he looks like a child now more
than a mate   he watches the cuban as long as he can and
then sits in a corner and is soon asleep

the cuban runs a hand over his face

> **i don know where we are now capn   i don**
> **know how long we been gon roun in circles**

the fog is a light gray so he knows it is daylight and he
knows it was black when he was last awake and he knows
even minutes off course can be ruinous

> **i keep it straight now capn   i keep it on course**
> **all a time**

wha   wha you hear

a lookout holds up a hand and turns an ear toward the
fog   others around him look confused but also lean
forward holding onto the lifeline and listening at the mist

the lookout raises and lowers his arm at the cuban

the cuban puts the engines into neutral and the boat
coasts forward until its momentum is exhausted

a weak murmur now swims to his ear

all rise in the boat

wha is it

a lookout leans farther over the boat

and the noise becomes louder

   and louder

      until it seems to have a physical presence of its
own   a deep gurgling growl that needs no body to carry
it and no mind to inspire it as the sound dissects the mist
and races across the sea   then a curtain parts and the
refugee ship roars within yards of the boat with its
engines howling and its rust patched by the fog and its
crew lying at odd angles about the deck with dried black
blood hanging from mouths and noses and ears and the
only movement a filthy white undershirt waving in the
fraudulent breeze from atop the bridge and the flapping
of huge wings as raptors hop from one meal to the next
clothed by the smell of decay that reaches out and
washes over the cuban and his crew

   oh god   oh no

and the ship is gone

these people need help   too many sick

the cuban looks back at his disintegrating cargo and then
to the unrelenting gray universe before him

the sea is a flat sheet of iron   dense and immobile
paralyzed by its own mass   trapped by its own
burden   too old and too tired and too pitiless to allow
another life to escape its grasp   the refugees are left
with the sound of their own whispers and scratchings
and timid movements accompanied by the bubbling
coughs that are another constant in this unchanging
world of gray on gray on gray

the cuban senses movement on deck but refuses to turn
around   he taps his gauges and touches his helm and
wipes a hand across his forehead but will only rotate his
head enough to see the teenager who sleeps curled in a
corner with his mouth parted and his hands between his

legs and his bare feet draped over the bridge   the cuban
can smile at this   he looks forward and waves at the
lookouts who lean against the lifelines and search for
objects in the sea or sounds from the earth and pass the
slightest stub of a cigarette from hand to hand and mouth
to mouth without a word or groan to break the silence

a wave passes under the boat

the engines groan for more fuel

a body is dropped into the sea

the cuban lifts his head from his arms and runs a hand
over his face to be sure of his surroundings   his fingers
tremble as he starts the engines and taps each gauge and
wipes the compass with the tail of his shirt   he looks up
again to be certain that what he sees is true and then
presses the throttle forward so carefully it seems the boat
will never move   that it will never part the sea as it did
before   but once past idle speed his confidence grows so
he presses on toward a speed only dreamed of and a land
that now seems imagined

on deck the vibrating diesels stir the fallen bodies into
motion   they rise slowly to their feet and stretch their
arms to the sky and wipe the sleep from their faces as the
wind dances across the rags they call clothes and removes
the stench of death from their bodies   they manage to
smile and even laugh as they shake hands and embrace
and gesture at the earth made moveable again   in their

midst an old man rummages through his possessions
until he uncovers a small plastic bag from which he
withdraws an unopened bottle   he holds it at eye level
for all to see as he breaks the seal with great ceremony
before passing it from hand to hand without having
sampled its contents himself   and on the bow the
lookouts laugh as a wave plows into the boat breaking
into hundreds of long white fingers that surge over the
lifelines and bathe them in salt and spray

the teenager places a hand on the cubans hard shoulder
marvelling at the movement on deck and the clearness of
his sight and the height of the gauges that seemed
condemned to uselessness just hours ago

the movement of the boat and the refugees and the sea
confirms the living even as a frail body is dumped over
the side taking with it an old greek fishermans cap and a
pair of shattered glasses to the bottom of the sea where it
will feed the cycle of life that moves with its own agenda

there are tears for the living and tears for the dead and
tears for the past and future as all eyes look to the east
and the dawn of a day and the light of the sun

the light of the sun

the end

Made in the USA
Columbia, SC
20 November 2024